INSIDE

OUTSIDE

UPSIDE DOWN

INSIDE

OUTSIDE

UPSIDE DOWN

by Stan and Jan Berenstain

A Bright & Early Book

RANDOM HOUSE/ NEW YORK

Going in

Inside

Inside a box

Upside down

Inside a box
Upside down

Going out

Outside

Outside
Inside a box
Upside down

Going on

On a truck
Outside
Inside a box
Upside down

Going

Going to town
On a truck
Outside
Inside a box
Upside down

Falling off

Off the truck

Coming out

Right side up!

Mama! Mama!
I went to town.
Inside,
Outside,
Upside down!